Goldilocks and the THREE BEARS

WRITTEN BY RENEE BIERMANN

ILLUSTRATED BY ROMÁN DÍAZ

DISCOVER DG GRAPHICS

PICTURE WINDOW BOOKS
a capstone imprint

Published by Picture Window Books, an imprint of Capstone
1710 Roe Crest Drive
North Mankato, Minnesota 56003
capstonepub.com

Library of Congress Cataloging-in-Publication Data
Names: Biermann, Renee (Author), author. | Díaz, Román (Illustrator), illustrator.
Title: Goldilocks and the three bears / by Renee Biermann ; illustrated by Román Díaz.
Other titles: Goldilocks and the three bears. English.
Description: North Mankato, Minnesota : Picture Window Books, an imprint of Capstone, [2022] | Series: A Discover Graphics fairy tale | Audience: Ages 5–7. | Audience: Grades K–1. | Summary: Goldilocks finds a special place in the woods, where she helps herself to food and falls asleep.
Identifiers: LCCN 2021006158 (print) | LCCN 2021006159 (ebook) | ISBN 9781663909022 (hardcover) | ISBN 9781663920911 (paperback) | ISBN 9781663908995 (ebook pdf)
Subjects: LCSH: Graphic novels. | CYAC: Graphic novels. | Bears—Fiction.
Classification: LCC PZ7.7.B4927 Go 2022 (print) | LCC PZ7.7.B4927 (ebook) | DDC 741.5/973—dc23
LC record available at https://lccn.loc.gov/2021006158
LC ebook record available at https://lccn.loc.gov/2021006159

Designed by Kay Fraser

WORDS TO KNOW

bushes—plants that grow close to the ground and have many leaves

odd—unusual or unexpected

swing (noun)—a kind of chair that hangs above the ground

swing (verb)—to move back and forth

Printed and bound in the USA. 4270

CAST OF CHARACTERS

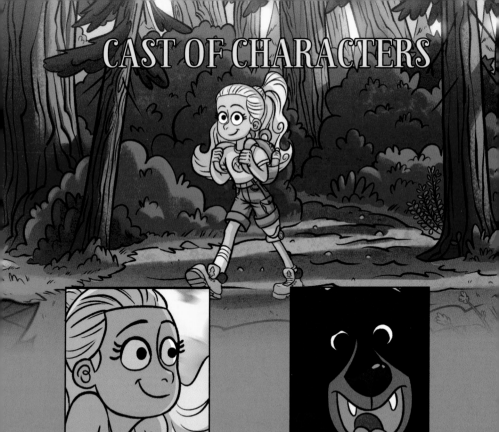

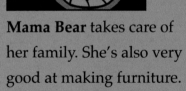

Goldilocks loves nature. She likes to go for walks in the forest. Sometimes, Goldilocks can be clumsy!

Mama Bear takes care of her family. She's also very good at making furniture.

Sister Bear is kind and welcoming. She makes friends easily.

Baby Bear is little and very cute. He likes to play.

HOW TO READ
A GRAPHIC NOVEL

Graphic novels are easy to read. Boxes called panels show you how to follow the story. Look at the panels from left to right and top to bottom.

Read the word boxes and word balloons from left to right as well. Don't forget the sound and action words in the pictures.

The pictures and the words work together to tell the whole story.

Once upon a time, Goldilocks went for a walk in the forest.

Goldilocks thought she saw something odd on the other side of the bushes.

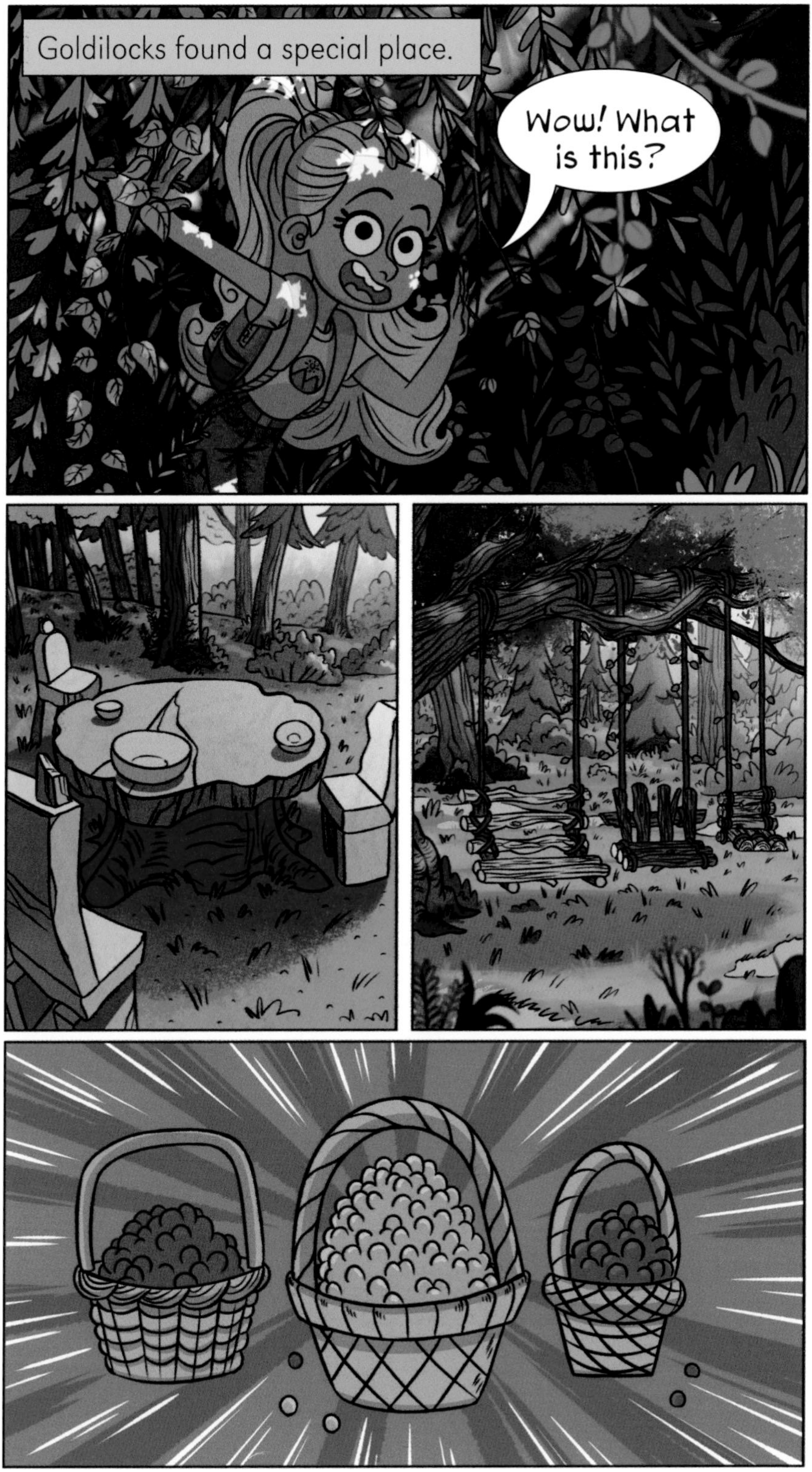
Goldilocks found a special place.
Wow! What is this?

Goldilocks saw some berry bushes and baskets of berries.

Goldilocks tried a yellow berry.

This berry is too sour!

Goldilocks tried a purple berry.

This berry is *too sweet!*

Goldilocks tried a red berry.

Yum!

This berry is just right!

Goldilocks ate all of the red berries.

Goldilocks saw some rock chairs.

Goldilocks tried the first rock chair.

This rock chair is too low.

Goldilocks tried the second rock chair.

This rock chair is too high!

Goldilocks broke the second rock chair.

Goldilocks tried the third rock chair.

This rock chair is just right!

Goldilocks saw some swings.

I want to swing!

18

Goldilocks tried the first swing.

This swing is *too big!*

Goldilocks tried the second swing.

This swing is *too* small.

Goldilocks tried the third swing.

This swing is just right!

21

Goldilocks liked the swing.

Soon, she fell asleep.

ZZZZ...

Just then, Mama Bear, Sister Bear, and Baby Bear arrived. They had been out for a walk.

The bears were surprised to see what had happened!

Goldilocks woke up and saw the bears.

I'm so sorry, bears. I will make it better!

She realized the bears were upset.

Mama Bear had an idea!

Thank you, Mama Bear. This swing is truly just right!

WRITING PROMPTS

1. How is this version of "Goldilocks and the Three Bears" different from other versions you've heard? Make a list of the differences you noticed.

2. Imagine that the bears in this story could talk. What would they say? Pick a panel they appear in and write down what you think they would say or think in that scene.

3. What do you think happens after the very last panel of the story? Write a paragraph describing Goldilocks's next adventure with the bears!

DISCUSSION QUESTIONS

1. Goldilocks feels bad when she realizes the bears are upset. When have you done something you felt bad about? How did you make it better?

2. What is something else the bears could build for their special place? How should they make it?

3. Do you think Goldilocks will visit the bears again? Why or why not?

DRAW A BEAR DEN

In real life, black bears can sleep outside on the ground or in underground dens. Imagine the bears in "Goldilocks and the Three Bears" have their own underground den in the forest. What do you think their den would look like?

WHAT YOU NEED:

- markers
- poster board
- construction paper
- scissors
- glue
- decorations like stickers

WHAT YOU DO:

1. Draw a large circle on the poster board. This will be the den.

2. Draw an opening for the den. Make sure the opening is big enough for Mama Bear to get inside!

3. Draw three leaf beds or make them from construction paper. Make sure each leaf bed is the right size for each bear. Label the beds: Mama Bear, Sister Bear, and Baby Bear.

4. Decorate the den to make it seem like a fun home. Use construction paper, stickers, and your imagination!

5. Show your den to a friend. Explain what is in the den and why.

READ ALL THE
AMAZING
DISCOVER GRAPHICS BOOKS

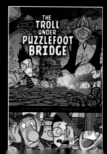